Foley, Winifred

To kill for
love / Winifred
Foley
LP

1771729

TO KILL FOR LOVE

WINIFRED FOLEY

LARGE PRINT
Oxford

First published in Great Britain 2006
by ISIS Publishing Ltd.

Published in Large Print 2006 by ISIS Publishing Ltd.,
7 Centremead, Osney Mead, Oxford OX2 0ES
by arrangement with
the Author

Foley, Winifred,

To kill for love
/ Winifred Foley

LP

The moral r 1771729   een asserted

British Library Cataloguing in Publication Data
Foley, Winifred, 1914–
    To kill for love. – Large print ed.
    1. Dean, Forest of (England) – Fiction
    2. Romantic suspense novels
    3. Large type books
    I. Title
    823.9'14 [F]

ISBN 0-7531-7654-8 (hb)
ISBN 978-0-7531-7655-9 (pb)

Printed and bound in Great Britain by
T. J. International Ltd., Padstow, Cornwall

The village chapel has no graveyard; villagers must go to rest in the churchyard two miles away. Many of the graves have headstones and those that haven't are neatly trimmed and in season have their jam jars of flowers, but in a corner there's one grave with an unreadable headstone, overgrown with weeds and the grass never tended. A wild rose has seeded itself there and tries to ramble over the neglect. The identity of the remains that lie beneath are often pondered by those with romantic ideas

.

CHAPTER
ONE

Around the year of 1890 it would have been difficult to find a more delightful activity than walking along a woodland path in the beautiful Forest of Dean on a summer's day. The leaves of the magnificent oaks provided a dappled shade. The tapestry of ferns and spires of brilliant foxgloves that carpeted the ground below the trees enchanted the eyes; the sweet twittering of birds was music to the ear, while the agile capers of a red squirrel added to the pleasure. This ancient oak forest had once been a Royal hunting ground, where deer and wild boars abounded. Then many of the oaks were cut down to make the ships that helped to conquer so much of the world. The forebears of those oaks now provided the coal on which the forest economy depended.

The thousand of acres of woodland were dotted with little villages of primitive stone cottages where the miners lived. Miners who were paid a pittance for their efforts, delving deep below ground for the black coal for the mine-owners who grew fat on their efforts. Above in the sun, little towns and an occasional farm were to be found amongst the trees in the lands intersected by the rivers Wye and Severn.

The villages were like little worlds of their own in which the inhabitants of about two hundred souls would demonstrate all the many characteristics of the human race. There were joys and fears, hatreds and loves, anger and laughter, while tragedies and traumas were frequent visitors in their lives. Each others' lives provided their entertainment. They laughed until they cried at the foibles of the eccentric and feckless and wept at the tragic evens inherent to any community. In village life individuality is emphasised, unlike the teeming nonentity of city life. From chapel minister to village simpleton, everybody was somebody; though some were more somebody than others.

In one of these little villages, which straggled up a steep slope from the main road, all the tiny drab stone cottages had little stone pigsties at the bottom of the garden near to the bucket "privy", adding to the odours. There were unpaved woodland paths to the village well, the school and a nearby farm. For transport the villagers depended on their legs, or perhaps a bicycle for the more affluent. Generally doors were never locked and people had little privacy. Rumours with a germ of fact abounded; if one started at the top of the village, by the time it had travelled down one side and up the other, it had been embellished out of recognition.

It was a true and tragic rumour when Sam Wilce had a severe stroke which left him paralysed down his right side and unable to talk properly. Sam and his wife Harriet kept the village post office and sold basic grocery items as well as tobacco and sweets, though any profit made on the latter was swallowed up by those too poor to pay their way. However, their cottage had a large garden which Sam planted from corner to corner. He also acted as insurance agent to the Prudential, walking miles once a week to collect the moneys. This meant the two of them could live in comfort. Their great regret was their childlessness, but this was in part made up by the great love shown to them by the village children.

Thus Sam's stroke sent waves of sympathy and grief through the village. Harriet was devastated, but there was a long-term chance that Sam would improve, and there were plenty of willing helpers to try and rub his useless arm back into life with goose grease. Harriet was desperately worried that they would lose their jobs but a letter from her brother in Wales brought great comfort. Her brother was a miner in Tredegar in South Wales, with eight children, six of whom were married, leaving at home one son and the youngest daughter, Eirwhin. Eirwhin had been born a sickly child, with a heart murmur but all the care lavished on her meant she had led an almost normal childhood and had grown up a bright and beautiful girl. Her parents refused to let her go into domestic service as her sisters had done and being clever, she had found work as a clerk in the local post office near her home, which was bigger than that of her Uncle Sam. However, hearing about her uncle's disaster, and ready for a change of scene, she was quite happy to come and work for them as she had always loved the holidays spent in the Forest.

Her presence and efficiency solved Harriet's problem but she certainly created a problem for all the eligible (and some ineligible) village males, for she was charming, chatty and had a roguish sense of humour. As so often happens, the winner in the race was the handsomest, most personable young man, Jim Roberts. He was a nice steady sort of chap with remarkably little conceit at 21 years old. In some people's eyes he was perhaps a bit too steady. This was put down to the fact that he was an only child of elderly parents — it had been a miracle that he had been born at all.

His mother had worked as a cook in a Gloucestershire manor house where his father was the groom. When Ellen, a pleasant homely type who had resigned herself to spinsterhood at the age of 39 years, had been engaged as cook, his father was already 50 years old. It was a bit of a joke among the young domestic staff when the two started to go out together. This changed to bigger and more ribald jokes when they married and Ellen moved in with him. It was past a joke when nature made it obvious that dour old John the groom was going to be a father. This also meant that they had to leave their jobs and move into a cottage in the Forest of Dean, where Ellen had some relatives. Age had served John meanly. Now in his seventies, he was crippled with arthritis, but Ellen still went to work in a bakery.

It was soon common knowledge that Jim and Eirwhin were an item. The more Jim saw of her, the more besotted he became. When things looked serious, Harriet told him in confidence about Eirwhin's heart murmur and emphasised that he must take extra care of her. It was therefore with some trepidation that she agreed to let Eirwhin and Jim do the insurance round. She tried to refuse, but Eirwhin was persistent. Harriet finally gave in, but didn't allow her to raise a finger in the house as well as working in the post office.

The walk, sometimes through lovely quiet glades, presented great temptation to these lovers. It became clear there was only one answer — they would get married. Apart from the other village girls who had a crush on Jim, together with their mothers, everyone thought is was a lovely idea. By great luck, George Berry, a blind 90-year old bachelor, died peacefully in his sleep leaving a cottage which was put up for sale at 80 sovereigns. Jim and Eirwhin had nearly twelve sovereigns saved up and Uncle Sam and Aunt Harriet provided the wedding meal and another five guineas. When Eirwhin's family came from Wales for the wedding, they contributed another five guineas as well as many useful presents. An agreement was reached over the price of the cottage, and the young couple moved in.

When they had been married a few months, Eirwhin began to want a baby, but having been warned by Sam and Harriet about the heart murmur, Jim would not risk it, not at any rate while she persisted in going to work. Sometimes the weather in winter made the insurance round impossible, but when they managed it, Eirwhin and Jim were often asked in to warm themselves by the fire. It fascinated Eirwhin how many women could make such cosy homes from such poor material, but where the black-leaded grate was shining, the hearth swept with a rag rug laid in front of the steel fender, the curtains drawn and the lamp lit in the middle of the table, these little homes were pleasant havens to enter. Some, however, where the family was large and money desperately short, were sad squalid hovels full of pale-faced hungry children. Eirwhin hated to take the insurance coppers from them, but the idea was to draw the money out when the daughters left school to go into service, to send them off tidy, with good shoes to their feet. On rare occasions, the policy was drawn out to bury the girls before they reached the age of 14 years of age. Occasionally Eirwhin and Jim paid the coppers in themselves but they could not make a habit of it. Eirwhin often thought of the family with three children about to sit down to what their mother described as "workhouse sop". To make this she boiled some onions and potatoes together, then mashed them up with a lump of lard or dripping, salt and pepper, and served the result on thick slices of white bread.

At another cottage, where two newly weds had moved in, the young wife was heavily pregnant. The husband's mother had given him his insurance book as a wedding present, which would provide a nest egg in a few years' time. Meanwhile they were managing with a table and chairs, a sack for a hearthrug, and stuck-on coloured paper at the windows instead of curtaining. For tea, a small tin of pineapple chunks had been divided between two saucers and two eggs were boiling in the pineapple tin on the fire. They didn't even own a saucepan. But they did have a rich expression for each other in their eyes. Eirwhin was full of admiration for the women who managed in such poverty and thought herself very lucky indeed.

As Christmas approached, it became known that a vaudeville troupe were coming to perform at the concert hall in the mining town two miles away. Those villagers who could scrape up the sixpence for the cheapest entry tickets were determined to go. It was a bitterly cold evening and few had topcoats, but the anticipation of the treat to come combined with beating their arms across their chests kept them going. Jim and Eirwhin were among them, Eirwhin well wrapped-up against the cold. Before they had set out, Jim had let their fire go low and shored it up with coals, lumps at the front and slack at the back. He left the guard in the front, knowing that when they returned, a few jabs of the poker would get a lovely blaze going. The paraffin lamps were filled ready for lighting and left on the table.

Once inside the warm crowded hall, the magic began. There were dancers, singers, a juggler, a contortionist, and a very good young comedian called Charlie Chaplin. They were all entranced. Emerging into the cold night air, full of good spirits, they sang, danced and joked their way home, for the show had exceeded their expectations. Even the chilly ones got warm climbing the steep lane on their way home, chattering about the performances they had just seen, comparing notes about the brilliance of the artistes. As they climbed, so people peeled away, calling goodnights, and there were only four of them left as they neared the top of the village: Joey and David, the nephews of Sam Wilce, and Eirwhin and Jim. Just yards from the cottage, Eirwhin suddenly stopped. "Oh God," she moaned and put her hand to her chest.

"What's the matter, darling, what's the matter?" Jim cried as he held her up. "Go in, boys, quickly, light the lamps and poke the fire, please!"

He picked Eirwhin up in his arms, but it was too dark for him to see her face swell up to a deep purple hue, then subside to the pallor of death.

Eirwhin, vivacious lovely Eirwhin was dead!

Carrying her in, Jim laid her on the sofa, groaning "No, no, darling, no!"

The alarmed boys ran to tell their neighbours and soon the little room was filled with weeping women and grey-faced men who, only minutes ago, had been full of laughter. Someone cycled to fetch the doctor. By the time he had come, Jim was in a state of shock. Harriet had come in and kneeling down by the sofa, she too had cried out, "No, no, Eirwhin!" Kissing the dead girl's hand she moaned, "This will kill my poor Sam. And my poor brother, this will break his heart." Leaning her head on Eirwhin's arm, she wept.

The doctor came and confirmed the death. Jim's state of mind was also considered, and considering that he might be in danger of taking his life, the doctor provided a strong dose of laudanum and asked that the men keep a close watch, not leaving him on his own.

He would arrange for Jim to be taken into care on the morrow, which would mean the asylum in the city some 20 miles away. When the time came, Jim went with the male nurses like a robot, all the spirit knocked out of him. The chapel minister had been in to commiserate, and had been heard to say it would have been better if the Almighty had taken him too.

A couple of months later Jim came home, a broken man but no longer suicidal. A bitter reclusive figure but not bitter with his fellow human beings — he pitied all humanity. His mother wanted him to go home and live with them, but he felt that his company would only add to her burdens. His father crippled with arthritis was misery enough to put up with. Jim went back to work. He would not accept charity — charity was not for able-bodied men, it was for the old and the ill. From his free allowance of coal, he left a bucketful by each widow's door. He would keep company with the sick and the dying, and he wandered on his own a lot in the forest, smoking his pipe. One night, a couple of forceful mates cajoled him to come to the pub with them, but he just sat there with the tears running down his cheeks, unable to join their banter and camaraderie. After a couple of years of self-neglect, he was a shadow of his former self and his young head was well sprinkled with grey hair.

Poor Harriet gave up shop-keeping and the insurance round, and just managed the post office. Perhaps inspired by her need for him, Sam gradually regained enough feeling in his limbs to limp about and his speech returned almost to normal.

CHAPTER
TWO

If the village children had poor pickings inside their homes, the miles of forest outside were rich pickings for childhood pursuits. Toys from shops were rare acquisitions, but they had trees to climb, streams to paddle in, and the rubbish tips around the village provided things with which to play "shops" and "houses". Five stones of nearly the same size could be rattled around in a tin till they were smooth enough to play the game of "Five Stones" with. "Cat and Stick" was a popular pastime — a piece of wood about six inches long would be sharpened at each end. When tapped by a large stick, it would fly up in the air and a whack from the bigger stick would send it quite a long way. The child who could step out the distance in the least steps was the winner. Any bits of string, rope or old stocking could be tied together for a skipping rope. Sometimes the children's older sisters or aunties home on a visit would bring old tennis balls, discarded by their employers. These were treasures beyond price. The piece of hardened earth by each garden gate was used for "Hopscotch" and ball games.

But childhood days were over all too quickly; one day children playing in the woods, the next far away from home, the denizens of attics and basements, prisoners in caps and aprons among strangers that treated them as second-class human beings. It was a brutal emotional transfer.

When Anna Harris reached 14 years old, instead of sending her to the beautiful but snobbish town of Cheltenham some 20 miles distant, Anna became kitchen maid to the Rectory just three miles away which meant she could come home on half days off. An astute, nice, clever young girl, she was ambitious and by the time she was 20, she had risen to the position of cook and was becoming restless. She soon began reading the job adverts in the Rector's discarded *The Times* daily. She saw one for a cook general to share duties with a house/parlourmaid, looking after a lady author in a small, very convenient, flat in Knightsbridge, London. The wages quoted were nearly twice what she was being paid. On impulse Anna wrote and was surprised to be offered an interview, subject to references from her current employer. This left her with no option but to give in her notice. The Rector's wife offered her an equal wage but Anna's wings had started to flutter. London — so far away, and it sounded so exciting. In the hopes that Anna would not like London and would come back, the Rector's wife wrote her an excellent reference. Anna's mother went with her to London for the interview, and thought the lady author would be a very good employer. Anna got the job.

The lady was indeed a considerate employer who paid a higher wage than average and allowed her two maids as much time off as she could manage. It was not long before Anna fell in love with London. She became as passionate about this huge area of man's genius and caprice as she was about the genius of nature in her beloved Forest of Dean. Ten years later she was still in the same job and content with her life. She loved her annual two weeks' summer holiday, for which she went home in the Forest, spending every minute of it she could manage out walking in the forest, filling the big apron she had borrowed from her mother with kindling wood.

Although a little on the plump side, she was a very attractive young woman and had plenty of would-be suitors in the village — as well as now and again a hopeful milkman back in London — but she never seem tempted. Her parents were very proud of her but there was also a strong feeling of sadness, for time was hurrying by and with no sign of a husband they grieved that they might never have grandchildren.

As the two weeks always went by so quickly, Anna was overjoyed when one year her mistress gave her six weeks' paid holiday while she went to India to do some research for a new book she was hoping to write. It was unbelievable — six whole weeks to spend with her parents in her beloved habitat. During the first three days of this great holiday it rained continuously but nothing could dampen Anna's spirits. She spent her time helping her mother about the house and doing a big batch of baking, which her dad particularly enjoyed. Then the sun came out, the birds sang, the flowers lifted up their faces to say thank you and the forest became a sylvan paradise. On went one of her mother's capacious aprons and Anna was off gathering firewood under the trees. The contrast with London was so great that she felt grateful for her fate.

She had quite an apronful of kindling wood when she spotted a large limb fallen among the ferns that would saw into some nice logs to eke out the coal. She emptied her apron, managed to balance the log on her shoulders and started for home. It was so quiet and peaceful that it was quite a shock when she noticed the forlorn-looking figure of a man sitting on a tree stump smoking a pipe. When he realized she had seen him, he stood up, knocked out his pipe and said "Let me carry that for you. It's Anna Harris, isn't it?"

She blushed for she didn't recognise him, but he looked so pale and drawn, with sad sunken eyes, that she protested she could manage. As she said the words, something in his looks reminded her of the young and handsome Jim Roberts that she had known. Surely this could not be him! The shock of realization brought a lump to her throat and tears to her eyes. Jim Roberts had been such a handsome fellow with a physique to match and thick brown hair. All the young girls in the village including herself had been smitten by him. Her mother had written in her letters how badly he had taken his wife's death but Anna thought how deeply he must have suffered to become like this.

Anna's mother held that tea-leaves were good for roses and was just emptying the teapot by the rose at the cottage door as Anna and Jim approached. She hid her surprise at seeing Jim, saying to them both, "I'm just going to brew a fresh cup of tea, I'm sure you two could do with one."

"No, thanks," said Jim, putting the limb down and turning to go away. Emboldened by pity, Anna took hold of his arm.

"Oh no, you don't. You must come in and have a cup of tea and a piece of my home-made cake or I shall be insulted."

Reluctantly he turned and came with her, but he sat on a hard chair just inside the door, nervously twisting his cap in his hands. Anna took it from him and handed him a cup and a large wedge of cake. He hurriedly ate the cake and swallowed the hot tea, wincing as it burned his throat, before taking his leave.

"Oh, Mam," Anna cried out when he had gone, "I didn't know him! He's gone so grey and has become skin and bones."

"Aye, my wench, 'tis pitiful what 'appened to that lad. 'Tis a shame that poor Eirwhin ever came to live 'ere, and 'tis a miracle you got 'im to come and take that tea and cake. He doesn't seem able to mix with folks any more."

"Yes," Anna said, thoughtfully. "Mam, I know he's on early turn at the pit and when he comes home, I'm going to take him down a good cooked dinner."

A spark of hope grew in Anna's mother's breast. Maybe somewhere, in the not too far future, a grandchild might yet be theirs. She smiled broadly at the thought as she answered, "That's a good idea, love. If anybody could do with a bit of cooking it's that Jim Roberts."

As soon as he came home the following day, Anna was on his doorstep with a huge hot dinner and pudding on a tray. He remonstrated and said he must pay her.

"You can pay by coming to collect wood with me," she told him and left him to eat his meal. He quickly washed himself and changed out of his pit clothes before sitting down to what was a feast to him. He then washed the plates together, placed them on the tray and carried it carefully back to the Harris's, where he knocked shyly on the door. Mrs Harris opened it.

"That was a wonderful meal. Your daughter certainly can cook, Mrs Harris," he said, handing her the tray. Anna was ready and waiting with her mother's apron on, and they set off into the woods. Jim was very quiet and Anna tried to chat to him, but was wary in case she might say something to hurt his feelings. When they got back with a load of wood, he wasn't allowed to argue over the sandwiches, tea, and some cake.

"Mam's made some lovely brawn," she told him, "so I'll come with you and get your bait tin for some sandwiches to take to work."

"Oh please, I must pay," he begged.

"All right, we'll tell you the cost at the end of the week." She gave in, knowing it was best for his pride. The ploy worked well; soon Jim Roberts was being fed by Anna Harris, and every day, according to what shift he was on, they went gathering wood. Talk was soon rife in the village: "Well, fancy that, it looks as though Anna Harris have set her cap at Jim Roberts. It'll be a miracle if she can cheer him up, and what'll be the good with her going back to London?"

Anna knew Jim's heart wore a shroud of grief for Eirwhin; she respected his mourning, never using her femininity to intrude on it. Nevertheless, as the days went by, walking in the forest with Jim became the most important thing in her life. At the end of her six weeks the Harris's woodshed was full, Jim was two stone heavier, and the dull look in his eyes was lifting. And Anna knew she had fallen in love.

All her latent instincts as a wife and mother had come with the care of this saddened man and Jim had found the comfort of her company overwhelming. They had never even kissed but both knew they could not live without each other. When the day came for Anna to leave, Jim called to carry her box to the little station half a mile from the village. They left early, walking in a pregnant silence for most of the way. The place was empty and they sat on the only seat on the little platform. Suddenly Jim put his head in his hands, his voice breaking as he said, "Oh Anna, I can't bear you leaving, I can't live without you, Anna!"

Anna started to cry, sobbing out, "Oh Jim, I don't want to go, I shall miss you too much." She stroked the top of his head. Grasping her hands, he raised his head, looking at her with a tear-stained face. In a rush, he said, "Anna, will you marry me?"

Her heart leapt and her face flushed as she threw her arms around him, saying in a rush, "Oh yes, Jim, I'd love to. I'll give my mistress notice when I get home but she's been so good to me and I've just had six weeks' paid holiday so I shall give her three months' notice to find another cook. And while I'm away, you must have your food at Mam's, promise me that, Jim, or I won't give in my notice."

He promised.

By the time her train came in they had exchanged their first kisses and two lonely futures had died on the station platform.

CHAPTER
THREE

As she had promised, Anna gave her considerate mistress three months' notice. After one month, Jim could bear it no longer and wrote to say that he would visit London by train on Saturday and go home on Sunday. Anna booked him a room in a terrace of rooming houses not far away. Her mistress gave her permission for Jim to have his meals at the flat and gave Anna as much free time as possible to show him around.

The train journey to Paddington seemed never-ending. When it stopped Jim could not see the station for the size of it. How would Anna find him in all this bustle and throng? And there she was, five feet four inches of precious womanhood, all his. The hugs and kisses they exchanged sent a magic fusion through them, but the station soon brought them back to earth. Anna took charge.

"We'll go to a café and have a cup of tea, and then I'll take you to where I have booked you a room. Then we will have to hurry to my place as I got to have luncheon cooked by 2 o'clock. Miss Storm says you can have your meals with the maid and me, but there will still be time for us to go for a walk when I finish this evening and tomorrow she is going out to dinner, so I will have a half-day off before you go home.

"She is so good to me, Jim. I've told her that if she is ever in need of me for a few days, I would oblige. I hope you don't mind, dear."

Jim was a bit awestruck by his room. It had a carpet on the floor and a bathroom with a basin on the landing. "How much did this cost, Anna? I must pay."

"Don't be silly, dear. This is a cheap place and besides you've paid your fare. Jim, we are partners. What is mine is yours and vice versa."

"Oh Anna," he gathered her to him, "I am so happy I can't believe it!"

He was even more impressed with the Knightsbridge flat. The kitchen had a sink, a steel trimmed range and a huge dresser with shining brass pans and good china displayed. When Anna allowed him a peep into the drawing room, dining room and bathroom, he realized how the other half live. When luncheon was over, the washing up done and the kitchen its usual spruce self, Anna took Jim to see Buckingham Palace and then they walked back through Hyde Park to look at the Albert Memorial in all its golden splendour. On the Sunday, following their lunch, they went to Hyde Park to listen to the Coldstream Guards band give an open air concert. All the time the feeling of beautiful intimacy grew stronger within them. They then hurried back to the guesthouse in plenty of time to vacate Jim's room, and found they had an hour to spare.

"Shall I ask whether they can do us tea and toast?" asked Anna.

Jim dropped to his knees, his arms around her. "Oh, Anna," he beseeched.

As she looked down at his face filled with longing, her heart melted and whispering, "All right, Jim," she locked the door.

With infinite tenderness and desire, Jim took this 30-year-old virgin and they knew they had made a bond for life. Both cried with happiness and a tinge of sadness. Jim couldn't help but think of Eirwhin but he comforted himself that if there was a heaven, then Eirwhin was certainly in it, and if there was nothing, then he had not betrayed her. Anna had tasted happiness beyond belief. They walked to the station in a daze of contentment.

CHAPTER
FOUR

Whilst Eirwhin lived, Jim had kept every inch of the garden around their little cottage cultivated, but over the years it had become neglected and overgrown. Now setting it to rights again for Anna was a solace for his mind and body. From under the tangled undergrowth he retrieved fruit bushes and strawberry plants, and his only reason for going to the forest was to collect sheep droppings for manure. He gradually burned to ashes the huge mound of weeds and branches that had dropped from a gnarled old apple tree. Soon the garden was a weedless picture of neat rows of healthy vegetables and fruit bushes.

It was four months before Anna finally had been replaced and could leave her job. In the meantime, the whole village gloried in this turn of events and the subject of Jim and Anna's forthcoming wedding kept the women full of anticipatory gossip. It was certain that the Harrises would put on a good wedding for their only child. It was a pity that Anna had left it so late as there would probably be no grandchildren, but there you are.

★   ★   ★

Over the years, Jim's mother had come every so often to give his cottage a good clean out, so he was not surprised to find her there when he came home from work one day.

"I've not done you a dinner, son, as I know you have it at the Harrises, but I'll brew a cup and of tea whilst you get the pit dust off and change your clothes. Then I want you to go upstairs and see if you like the present me and your Dad bought you."

Jim went upstairs feeling very puzzled. Then he saw the iron bedstead with the brass knobs was gone. In its place was a new wooden bed. The framed photograph of Eirwhin which lived on the chest of drawers where he saw it every day had gone; looking in the top drawer, there it was. He knew his parents were right; he must let go of the past for Anna. He went downstairs and hugged his mother.

"It's lovely, Mam. Tell Dad I do appreciate it and I know Anna will."

Ellen gave a sigh of relief; she knew she had done right.

With the garden done, Jim with the help of Anna's mother set about decorating the inside of the cottage but it was Anna who, with a present of money from her mistress which, together with her own savings, came to a nice sum, added new curtains, rugs, pretty crockery, cushions, pictures and some ornaments, all of which turned it into a cosy little paradise in the village's eyes.

As people had foreseen, it was a no-stint wedding. Anna had given in to her mother's plea for a white wedding and eventually all was made ready. They married on a gloriously sunny day. After the simple ceremony, relations, neighbours and friends enjoyed a feast created through the cooking skills and generosity of Anna and her parents. The newly weds went to London for the weekend to stay in the hotel where Cupid had bonded them. From a figure of pity Jim had become a figure of envy to many.

Two years later, one evening Elizabeth Harris was fidgeting about, waiting impatiently for the clock to go round and her husband to come home from work. On his return, she followed him into the washhouse where warm water was waiting in the copper for him. She burst out, "Oh Jack, our Anna is expecting. She told me today she is four months gone. She has seen the doctor and everything seems all right. She just wanted to be sure before she told us. Jack, I am so happy!" and she sat on the stool by the wash copper and burst into tears.

"There, there," he said, putting his arms around her. "It be wonderful news, but we musn't get too excited. There's many a slip 'tween cup and lip. Let us hope to God that everything will be all right."

Five months later everything did go all right and Anna gave birth to a beautiful seven-pound baby girl. They named her Elizabeth Ellen after her two grandmothers, but it was soon shortened to Beth, and Beth she was called by everyone. When she was christened, the chapel was packed and the beloved old hymns were sung with more fervour than ever. By the time she was four years old, her cute little ways and doll-like appearance made her an object to be idolized by everyone. To please Anna, Jim even started to go to chapel again. He had become a happy man, relaxed in his relations with his work-mates, thoughtful of his parents and his in-laws, and deeply loving his "two ladies" as he called Anna and Beth. Apart from the grim nature of his work in the pit, life was idyllic for Anna and Jim.

They had become very fond of their neighbour "Granny" Crook and her seven-year-old grandson, Lenny, whom she was bringing up. Lenny was a gentle kindly little boy who was like a brother to Beth. Granny Crook was called "Granny" by the entire village. She had been widowed young when her miner husband died from the effects of too much coal dust on his lungs, a dreadful death common amongst the miners for which there was no cure. She had been left with three little daughters and Parish Relief gave her four shillings a week, which allowed her at least to survive. Jim Roberts had always left coal at her door.

All the girls had all gone into service at the age of twelve and been great supports to their mother, sending home all they could spare from their meagre wages. Alas, when she was only 17 years old, the youngest one, Becky, a very pretty girl, had started to keep company with a young milkman. One evening he took her home on his half-day. His mother, who had been there, went out to see a sick friend, temptation and nature took over and Becky became pregnant. Granny Crook had been terribly upset but tried not to scold too much and did not, like some desperate mothers, put her daughter in the workhouse for the birth and let the baby be adopted. Granny Crook helped the village midwife and suffered as her daughter went into a long labour. The baby was a boy and Granny Crook was besotted with him from the start. She was only too willing for her daughter to go back into service and leave the child, who was named Leonard, Lenny for short, for her mother to bring up.

Becky went back to work in the same big house on the outskirts of Birmingham. She and the milkman were still in love but had learned from their mistake and waited for three years to get married. Becky wanted to have Lenny back, but when she saw the grief it would cause her mother and the fact that Lenny was very happy with his grandmother, she let things be. She had two more sons, and because her husband finished his milk round early, for he started work at 4.00a.m., Becky could go out to cleaning jobs in the evening so that she could send her mother a weekly sum for Lenny's keep.

One lovely sunny morning in July, with the cottage doors and windows wide open, Anna was preparing Sunday dinner. Jim was gardening; he had brought her new potatoes, peas, broad beans, sage and onions for stuffing and a bowl of strawberries to share with Granny Crook. Both she and Granny Crook sat outside their cottage doors shelling peas and broad beans, exchanging comments while contentedly watching Beth and Lenny playing marbles on the little shared courtyard in front of the cottages. Anna hadn't much of a voice but she tried to sing out of the sheer happiness of her lot. They sat and chatted, popping in now and then to check the meat roasting in the oven until Granny Crook announced hers was done and called to Lenny to come, his dinner was ready. Lenny went indoors and soon after Anna told Beth to go and tell Daddy that Mammy was about to serve up the dinner.

Jim had said he intended to take out the gnarled old apple tree at the end of the garden as it took up a lot of room for the few apples it produced. Anna had warned him it would be a tough job, for it had been there as long as she could remember. He had already sawn off most of the branches, stacking them up to saw for fire logs, leaving only enough to form some leverage for getting the roots out.

Anna was straining a saucepan of boiling water over a dandelion that had seeded itself in a crevice by the cottage door when a puzzled Beth came back, saying "Daddy's sleeping, Daddy's laying down and I can't wake him up." A terrible feeling of apprehension came over Anna. Dropping the pan, she hurried on shaky legs down the garden, her heart racing as she saw the still form lying by the tree stump. She knew Jim was dead as soon as she saw the blank stare of death on his beloved face. He had fallen by the partly uprooted apple tree, his still burning pipe lying in the earth beside him. Anna fell to her knees, cradling Jim's still warm body, moaning "Jim, oh Jim!" Abandoned and shocked, Beth began howling, her cries soon bringing Granny Crook out to see what ailed the child. One glance told her all, and she sent Lenny off to fetch other neighbours. One of the men set off to run the couple of miles to the doctor's.

Granny Crook's cottage had a little parlour with a horsehair sofa in it. The men fetched a hurdle and placed Jim's body on it, carrying him into the cottage and laying out on the sofa. The women coaxed the stricken Anna indoors where her distraught parents tried to comfort her. Granny Crook had saved the dinner from burning but they could get no food down Anna's throat.

Eventually, the doctor came in his pony and trap, his face sad and drawn by the terrible news. After examining the body lying still in Granny Crook's parlour he went next door to see to Anna. Kneeling down at her side, he took her hands in his, saying, "I know just now you are feeling beyond comfort, Anna, but just remember — you have given Jim some wonderful years and he has died whilst he was a very happy man. Not a lot of us have that blessing, Anna, and he has left a beautiful daughter to keep his spirit alive. Try and be brave for her sake."

Choking from all her sobbing, Anna stammered, "But Doctor, he seemed so well!"

"Yes, my dear, but his body suffered from years of self-neglect. The pit is not the healthiest place to work and smoking that pipe of his will have done his lungs no good. His heart had been damaged and heaving at that old apple tree was too much for him. Now, I'll leave you something to help you sleep. Please try to take some nourishment. Anna, you will have to be the strong girl I know you are. You've got Beth to live for, while your parents, Jim's parents and your friends and neighbours are suffering for you. You must think of them too." He stroked her head gently and was gone.

Now Anna could really take the measure of Jim's grief over Eirwhin. She hoped there was a God above like they had taught her at Sunday School, and so great was her love for Jim that she hoped he was reunited with Eirwhin. This unselfish thought brought her a grain of comfort. Sunday dinner was the culinary highlight of the village week; even the poorest had meat for that meal, if only a cow's heart, but that day the food stuck in the throats of many, and more than one teardrop fell on dinner plates.

CHAPTER
FIVE

Man must die and woman must weep but those that's left must earn their keep, and so it was with Anna. She must keep going for the sake of Beth. Very soon after Jim's funeral, rumour in the village had it that the cook had given in her notice at a nearby mansion of the mine owner Sir James Benson and his wife. It was a ray of hope, for although it was a live-in job, Anna thought they might let her go daily. She knew it was normal practice for a cook to have time off between luncheon and dinner. This precious time could be spent at home with Beth. She could leave Beth at her mother's on the way to work, her mother would have Beth all day and then take her home, put her to bed, and sit with her until Anna returned. Now, if only she could get the job; rumour wasn't always fact. First she went to the woodsmen's cottages, where the cook's father, a local forester, lived, to find out what was happening.

These foresters' cottages were isolated, sometimes miles apart, but Anna never minded walking through the lovely forest. The isolation meant that she could pour out her heart to Jim's spirit and have the relief of tears run down her face. Removing the traces of her emotions as she neared the cottage, which had a well-planted garden, she knocked at the door. It was answered by a pleasant-looking woman in a clean white blouse and navy apron, surprised but very pleased to have a visitor. Anna thought how lonely these women's lives must be, especially when the children had left home. Anna knew her name was Mrs Browning and recognised her from the chapel, to which she had often come.

"Come inside," Mrs Browning greeted her. "I was just thinking of making myself a cup of tea. Perhaps you could do with one?"

The little living room was a picture of cosy welcome, with a kettle ready to start singing on the hob. Anna thought how lucky Mr Browning was to come home to this. Then she thought of Jim who would never come home again, and the tears welled up in her eyes. Mrs Browning bustled about making the tea and putting two plates down for a piece of cake each.

"Now, my dear, is there anything I can do for you?" she asked as she sat down.

"I've heard that your daughter is cook at Waterloo House and that she might be leaving, and I wondered if it was true."

"Yes, my dear, it is quite true. Not that there is anything wrong with the job. Lady Benson is a real lady, treats her people as people. But my other daughter in Wales was lucky to marry a man who's not short of a bob or two and they are buying a little place to take holiday guests. Seems there is a lot of profit in it. They want our Ada to be a partner in the business and do the

32

cooking. Well, our Ada has a bit put by herself and she is all for it. However good the mistress, it is much better to work for yourself."

"I'm an experienced cook, too. I have excellent references but I couldn't live in. You see, I have a little girl not five years old, but my mother would mind her whilst I was a work. I lost my husband recently, it was very sudden . . ." and Anna's voice choked on the words.

"Oh my dear, was he the miner who died in the garden trying to pull up an old apple tree?"

Anna's eyes filled with tears again as she tried to understand how she was at the centre of such an appalling story.

"Oh, I am so sorry. It's heartbreaking, and I know what it is to have your heart broken. We had a little son as well as my daughters. He used to go playing with the boys in the village. I never worried he would come to any harm. One day they all went to that pond by the brickworks. A couple of the older lads had learned themselves to swim and laughed at our Eric because he wouldn't go in the water. He watched the boys jumping in and swimming, and sick of being taunted, he jumped in instead of paddling at the edge with others who couldn't swim. My poor boy panicked and drowned, and I don't know how me and my poor husband lived through the misery of it. He was only eight years old. Now I take a bit of comfort in the thought that he might have had to join the army in the war and get killed or kill others, which I am sure would have plagued his mind. We may never get over these things, my dear, but time do help.

"Now, if I might offer you a bit of advice. I know Lady Benson have interviewed a couple of women who are after the job. Now you're here, it is no distance to the big house. If I were you, I would call there on your way home and ask if it be convenient to see Lady Benson. I know they are there this evening, and she can only say no, and there is no harm in trying. I do wish you luck, my dear." She put her arms around Anna's shoulders and kissed her on the cheek. This warm gesture and friendliness did Anna good and she decided to follow the advice.

A kitchen maid answered her knock on the servants' entrance. Anna explained that she was after the post of cook and wondered if Lady Benson would like to interview her at some time. The maid left her on the doorstep which she delivered the message. After what seemed an interminable age to Anna, a housemaid came to the door to say that Lady Benson would see her now.

She was ushered into what appeared to be a book-lined study where Lady Benson sat at a desk. Both women had a favourable impression of each other on first meeting. Invited to sit, Anna explained her position and the tragedy that had caused it. Apparently reports of Jim's death had reached the big house, and Lady Benson expressed her sympathy. She was a mother herself and could imagine how hard it would be to lose your husband and then have to live apart from your child.

"What experience have you had as a cook?" she asked.

Anna had her two references with her and Lady Benson was very favourably impressed. Having stated what rate of pay was being offered, she continued, "Obviously you are just the sort of person I am looking for, but it seems a lot for you to manage. You see, there would be long hours, 8.00 a.m. to 10.00 p.m. if we have guests for dinner. However, you would get time off from 2.30 to 4.30 every day, and when we go out for dinner, which is fairly frequent, you would finish for the day at 2.30. However, I must warn you that there would be days now and again when we entertain when you would have no time off during the afternoon. You must think it over."

"My lady, I am sure I could manage it. My mother is prepared to have my little girl Beth for all the hours I am at work, and I would be able to spend time with her most afternoons. I shall be glad of the activity to take my mind off my worries and to be able to spend nights at home with Beth would be wonderful."

"Well, I must say having a daily cook had never occurred to me, but I am willing to give you a month's trial. Cook leaves in nine days. Could you start then?"

"Yes, my lady."

"Right, then, I will take you to see Cook in the kitchen. I am very sorry to lose her, but you can have a chat with her about your duties. I expect she will tell you that my husband always likes his breakfast eggs cooked on both sides and his bacon very crisp; apart from which we're not too difficult to please."

"Thank you very much, my lady." Anna's relief and gratitude nearly made her curtsey, but Lady Benson merely smiled and led the way out of the room. The kitchen was big and pleasant, and the cook confirmed all that her mother had told Anna. This was a very good job. It was a very relieved Anna who hurried home and ate the meal her mother had prepared for her while she told her the good news.

Anna sometimes had a job to hold back the tears during the mile walk through the woods to work. "Oh Jim," she would sigh, and the branches of the great oaks around sometimes seemed to sigh with her in a breeze. She would pick leaves from the wayside to pat her red eyes, especially if they had dew or rain on them. Once indoors, with her cook's apron on, her duties occupied her mind. She was an excellent cook and used her talents to the full in gratitude for the job. The Bensons responded with compliments and a raise in her wages.

Sometimes when they had guests for dinner or a big house-party, it would be after midnight when she got home, but the exhaustion was a blessing that helped her to sleep. On those evenings when the Bensons went out to dinner, Anna could spend most of the day with Beth in her own cottage, treasured hours with just herself and her beloved daughter. Two years later she was still there.

Now she spent so much time with her grandma, Beth did not see so much of Lenny. He had formed a close friendship with Robin, a young hunchback his own age, with a twisted spine that made mobility painful and difficult. Both lads treated Beth as a little sister and shared any playtimes they could. Nature had made some redress to Robin for he was exceptionally intelligent and sensitive, with a wonderful appreciation of beauty and any music that came his way. The villagers accounted for his cleverness by the fact his father was a love child born to a young domestic from the forest who had fallen for the charms of one of the young boarders at the Cheltenham College for Boys.

Now and again Nature, in her infinite variety, will produce a real live Venus, often in the most unlikely places. So it was with Dora Johnson, the eldest child of seven from a pair of unprepossessing parents. She was a real beauty. At fourteen years old and unaware of her potential, she had got a job at the college. To the young students, the maids were just capped and aproned cogs in the machine of domesticity. They cleaned the rooms, made the beds and put the food on the tables, and were beneath notice as females. That was until Dora was promoted to parlourmaid and waited on the tables. A cap and apron could not disguise her face and figure and she became a subject of much admiration, especially to a swarthy, handsome, hot-blooded seventeen-year-old, Colin Rathbone, son of a senior member of the Indian Civil Service, whose eye was caught by Dora as she walked out for her half-day. The sight of her in a cotton dress which was modestly cut but did little to hide her figure, rather emphasising it as she walked, aroused his interest and on impulse he decided to follow her. All he knew was that her name was Dora.

She walked into town and stopped to look in a sweet shop window before going in. He followed her into the shop, where there were several customers waiting to be served. He stood beside her, and as she turned her head, he smiled and said, "Hello, it's Dora, isn't it? Let me buy you some sweets." She recognised him from the college and was shocked but flattered that he had spoken to her, although she was sure it wasn't officially allowed. She blushed and demurred, buying herself some toffees. He ignored her and bought a large box of chocolates, thrusting them into her hands.

Dora was sixteen and had never had a boyfriend. Despite listening to the gossip of the other maids, she knew little of the ways of men, for her innocent nature had made the maids reserved in their chatter. Her idea of romance came from novelettes, and now it seemed that what was happening to her was like what happened in her favourite reading matter. The fact that this handsome stranger had a slight accent made it all the more exciting.

Escorting her out of the shop, he asked, "Where are you going now?"

"Oh," she murmured, her face flushing, "I was going to the park to see the band play."

"What a good idea! I'll join you, if I may," and they set off together. Finding a bench near the bandstand, they sat and listened for a bit. After sitting a while, he said, "Please, let us have some chocolates."

Blushing for her lack of manners, she gave him the box to open. As they ate their way through the chocolates, he told her about his childhood in India, his mother's early death, the reaction of her family, and the way in which his father had decided his only son must go to England to learn about his father's world. Dora was enthralled by the romantic story and soon was chatting freely. Suddenly though he jumped up.

"I must hurry back to college," he said. "I have some studying to do." He kissed her on the cheek and hurried away.

On getting back to her room Dora looked in the mirror, asking the flushed reflection she saw, "Did that really happen to Dora Johnson?" Yes, she thought, I am pretty, and a little voice inside said, "I hope he won't forget me."

The town of Cheltenham is a very lovely one, with wide tree-bordered streets, glorious parks, and noble Georgian houses built when it was a spa. There were many leafy glades suitable for young lovers and Colin took Dora to them. He dared too much when he took her one evening on her half-day off to see a famous play at the theatre. The headmaster of the college was taking his wife to the theatre on the same night and they had seats a couple of rows behind the couple. It was obvious that one of his pupils was courting a girl, and one that he recognised as on the domestic staff of the college. Colin was expelled and it was not long after that Dora's clear condition earned her the sack.

Their brief illicit dalliance produced Robin's father. Dora's parents were so angry with her — she had got herself into this trouble, they had no room nor means to cope with a baby, and they had no redress against the perpetrator. However, they allowed her to have the baby at home and found a kindly childless couple to adopt him. Named Timothy, he grew into a handsome, slightly swarthy, boy. At fourteen years, he started in the pit, for his adoptive parents were poor people. However, they left him their cottage when they died, one close on the other, and at first he bore the heartache, going to the pub and drinking cider of which he was too fond.

Luckily for him, Jane Tingle came home for the holidays from her domestic service and attracted his attention. She was a very sensible, wholesome sort of girl, they were soon married, and she bore him two sons; he learned to keep his cider drinking under control. Jane also became the local wise-woman and herbalist, having a real talent for this.

When the younger of the two boys was seven years old, Jane got pregnant again. Timothy had a great longing for a daughter, and so great was his belief that this time Jane was going to achieve it, he gave up cider altogether. His disappointment when she produced a delicate crippled baby boy drove him into depression and back to the cider. It ruined his liver and killed him in his late forties. Jane grieved, but Robin became the beloved centre of her universe. His intelligence was soon obvious. From her slender earnings as an amateur nurse, fruit-picker and general help, she bought Robin a very old cottage organ and he taught himself to play by ear to a very high standard. Although humanist by belief, he went to chapel to please his mother and played the organ there on occasion. He was by far the best pupil in the Dame school in the village, and was called upon to read the letters for those in the village who could not read or write. Before long, he and Lenny became like brothers.

CHAPTER
SIX

Despite the efforts Anna put into her job, her garden flourished with all the help from her father. Now she was looking forward to a busy two weeks in her own cottage and garden whilst Sir James and Lady Benson were on holiday in France. The groom's wife, who also helped in the kitchen, would have the job of preserving the soft fruit from the big house kitchen garden. Meanwhile, the groom, Alf Turner, had an exciting new duty. The squire had bought a car, a huge black shining monster. And he was to have lessons to drive it. Someone said he looked a proper gentleman in his chauffeur's suit and peaked cap. A new hard surface had been laid on the half-mile drive from the main road to the big house.

Anna felt like a privileged lady herself with soft fruit to pick from her own garden to make jam for herself and Beth and to share with her parents and Granny Crook. Taking advantage of a lovely warm sunny day, she set out to harvest the luscious berries. Lenny and Robin had gone down to Robin's house so Beth took her sewing box and sat on the grassy bank under shade of the oak across from the cottage, making a doll's dress.

Anna had returned to the house and was about to weigh two colanders of strawberries when she heard some piercing screams from Beth. Dropping fruit and bowl, she dashed outside where she saw three lads running away into the woods. Rushing across the road, she found Beth, her treasure, her darling, with blood streaming down her face and one eye hanging down on her cheek. Anna's own hysterical shrieks brought the horrified neighbours round. One man ran for the doctor but it was Bill Hatton, the cobbler, who ran like a mad man to the big house and told Alf Turner what had happened. "Drive her to the 'ospital, Alf, 'tis a 'ospital job I be afeared."

Without a second's thought of the outcome, possibly the sack, Alf drove to the bottom of the village where Anna and her parents, Lenny, Robin and Robin's mother were standing, with Beth cradled in her Granddad's arms. With Beth, Anna, and her parents, he drove to the hospital in Gloucester City 20 miles away with all the speed he could dare. He didn't pass another car on the way, but left a few scared horses startled on the road.

Starched aproned nurses took the shocked but now quietened Beth from her mother's arms. Anna and her parents, grey-faced and stunned, put their arms round each other.

"Oh God, oh God, what have I done, Dad, for this to happen?" Anna wailed.

"Nothing, my wench," her father sobbed and in his agony he raised a clenched fist heavenwards. They waited in stricken silence till a doctor came out to them.

"First," he said, "I can tell you that your little daughter will be all right. She is a bonnie child and a credit to you. But I've also got bad news. We will have to keep her in for a couple of weeks. Her face will be badly bruised for some time but fortunately there are no bones broken. However, she has lost the sight in both her eyes."

Anna looked at him and promptly fainted. Smelling salts and water soon brought her round and nurses came with a cup of tea and sandwiches, telling Anna she would soon be able to see Beth. Only Alf ate the sandwiches, but the tea was welcomed by all. When finally Anna was allowed to see Beth, who lay with her eyes bandaged and the rest of the face going black with bruising, she was much distressed. The child was unconscious after being anaesthetized, and nothing would persuade Anna to leave her bedside.

Anna's father took Alf aside and said, "You can see the way it is, Alf. The only thing is for her mother and me to get home and pack some things for Anna to stay near this hospital 'til Beth is discharged. I will take the responsibility to see Sir James and tell him that I persuaded you to use the car. But would you drive us in again tomorrow?"

Alf nodded, too near to tears himself to speak.

That night the hospital provided Anna with a nightdress and dressing gown and put her bloodstained clothes into a bag for her mother to take home. She spent the night tossing and turning on the hard bed as she mourned for her child's lost sight. The next day her parents came in early with fresh clothes and she set about finding a room to rent near the hospital. She was allowed to spend her days by Beth's bedside, talking to her of all the things at home that she must look forward to on her return, and preparing herself for the long struggle she saw ahead. The doctor said that he had never seen so quick or good a recovery. In two weeks she was ready to go home, but without those jewels that can say so much as well as see.

They went home by train, with Anna guiding Beth to the station in town and on the walk from the little local station half a mile from the village.

"It fair took my 'eart to see 'em," commented a villager who had seen them come through the woods, with Beth in her black spectacles walking gingerly instead of running ahead.

The Bensons had returned, and Anna's father had been up to see them, explaining how desperate things had been. There was no reprimand for either Alf or Anna, but a good deal of sympathy and a message for Anna that they would manage with the kitchen maids and the groom's wife until she came back. And that if she wanted to bring Beth to work with her sometimes, she could. Also, that if they were entertaining and needed Anna's time, a servant's bedroom would be at their disposal. Deeply grateful for the consideration shown, Anna gathered her broken spirit together, and with the intense love for her handicapped child summoned strength to carry on — but she often wondered what sort of future lay ahead for Beth.

CHAPTER
SEVEN

Matt Warden came into the world in a rush, tearing his mother in the process, weighing nearly eleven pounds, a good deal bigger than any other village baby. He went at his mother's breast with greedy energy and grew up into a short, broad, powerful man with three insatiable desires, food, sex and hard work. He was like a stud animal thinly disguised as a man, and full of animal magnetism. Eyebrows shot up when he started courting and then married Ethel Chivers, a sedate ladylike chapelgoer, the only child of an elderly couple who kept a shop in a village a couple of miles away. As more than one villager commented, "Still waters run deep." He kept her permanently pregnant; she was soon expecting their fourth child, and was by then a drab careworn sample of her former self.

They did not go short, however. He did all the work available at the pit, kept a flock of sheep on the free grazing in the forest, had fowls and pigs, selling his surplus eggs, and cultivated a huge garden. All these activities, as well as his conjugal rights, did not damp down his sexual appetite. Most of the village women avoided him. They were made uncomfortable by the way his eyes summed them up as possible conquests.

One or two of the flighty ones obliged him on the sly and a finger was rightly pointed at him when poor simple Holly had still-born twins. The authorities put her in a home away from further temptation, leaving him free to cool his carnalities where he could.

It was very rare, except in marriage, for anyone to move into the village. So when they did they were objects of intense interest and speculation and, in the case of Dorothy Dowell and her three children, a good deal of sympathy. Even the poorest in the village knew the luxury of being sorry for someone worse off than themselves. As a child, Dorothy Dowell had been an unpopular snobbish girl and had thought herself very superior when she landed Leslie Dowell for a husband. No miner for her, but a skilled stonemason who often worked away from home restoring old abbeys, cathedrals and grand manor houses.

But when the fancy took him he was also a skilled seducer of women, for he was a handsome man with sleepy long-lashed blue eyes, sly and quiet in his ways. For years his dalliances away from home had kept them temporarily short of necessities. Dorothy had borne him three children before she became bitter and disillusioned with their marriage, but though mortified by his behaviour, pride had made her put a brave face on things until recent years when not only did he stop coming home, he stopped sending any of his wages and forwarded no address for her to write to.

In a desperate attempt to hide her plight from her neighbours, she went to the police to trace him and she had to apply for Parish Relief. They granted her seven shillings a week, her rent being three shillings a week. Somehow, through a mutual distant relative, she arranged lodgings with an elderly deaf and dumb couple in the village for one shilling and sixpence per week. This would give her the use of a small bedroom and landing and the back kitchen, a fairly large room, which housed the wash copper and the coal. She borrowed a handcart, and with her children's help pushed it one and a half miles through the wood with their few pitiful belongings. Into this squalid cottage the Dowells moved, but as long as she had access to water, and as well as rainwater there was a well nearby, nothing could reduce the high standard of cleanliness Mrs Dowell achieved.

It was almost an aberration. Her marriage had gone sour and her world felt unclean, and scrubbing everything on hand was a sort of exorcism. The wash copper was her god; she and the children were always carrying water to fill it. Pennies for soap and soda she would always spare and there was always plenty of free wood in the forest to heat the copper. She partitioned off the coal with a piece of zinc she had found, and then scrubbed the coal-blackened flagstones until they were clean enough to eat off.

The children were thin, inadequately fed, shabbily clothed but they and their clothes were models of cleanliness. Every night she scrubbed her three offspring in the zinc bath she had brought with her. She was stick-thin herself, tight-lipped and kept herself to herself. She cleaned the filth and muddles out of her hosts' cottage and they repaid her with bits from their garden. She cooked on the old couple's grate and soon had it blackleaded and shining as a fat black man's cheeks; such drastic hygiene was a novelty in the village.

The two older children were just coming up to fourteen years old: a girl, Kitty, and a boy, Ernest. The other boy, David, was only a year younger. She did not want the boys to go down the pit, bringing coal dust and cockroaches home but there was little else they could find in the way of employment. She got hold of a newspaper and found them both a job as living-in gardener's boys on a country estate near Bristol. In her way, Dorothy Dowell loved her sons, but she did not love, nor even like, Kitty. She was too much like her father, sly, quiet and enigmatic, and also exquisitely beautiful.

Robin did not like going to Chapel, he had a questioning mind which looked sceptically at the tales told in Sunday School or the categoric statements of the chapel sermons; he went to please his mother who had great comfort from her Christian faith. As well as intelligence, Robin had a profound appreciation of beauty in all its forms, in music, what art came his way, and his surroundings. In the summer as he walked up the garden path he never failed to stand and stare at the large red velvety climbing rose against the grey stone wall of the cottages, or at the way the sunlight picked out the foxgloves to a queenly radiance among their courtier ferns.

At 18 years old, romantic notions filled his soul, though he has sure that he would never find anyone to satisfy his longings. He knew his twisted body would never get him a mate, but he indulged in daydreams about Mary Pickford, the screen's sweetheart. Then one Sunday, 14-year-old Kitty Dowell came to chapel and sat in the pew next to him. Dressed in a faded felt hat and shabby dress, the other village lads would have rejected her on sight, but Robin thought her the most exquisite human being he had ever seen. Her skin flushed with the walk to the chapel had him think of the wild roses growing on the quarry top, her delicacy matched the fragile beauty of their petals that fluttered to the ground if one went to pick them. Her mouth was a perfect cupid's bow, topped by a neat nose and a pair of deep blue eyes with dusky long lashes. Her long fair hair was shiningly clean.

Robin dared to smile at her, and she smiled back, not put off by his twisted body. For this smile he gave her his heart and then the two paper wrapped humbugs his mother always put in his pocket She took them and the little chapel seemed to have turned into paradise. He knew he could never be her sweetheart but her smile gave him permission to make her the object of his romantic daydreams.

Not long after this, matters began to improve for the Dowells. Mr Dowell had been traced by the police and his wife had applied for help in obtaining support from him. Although he didn't return to the family, he was ordered to send some of his wages regularly to his wife. Another cottage had become available in the village as old Ginny Hopkins had to go into the workhouse. Her mind was going, she was no longer safe on her own, and her family were too poor and hard-pushed to take care of her. Over the years her senility and lack of means led to the cottage being grossly neglected. It was a treasure trove of hard work and gallons of hot soapy water. Dorothy Dowell was in her element for a while. Kitty left school to work in the small mining town two miles away, in a newsagent's and tobacconist's shop, with the good wages of five shillings a week, dinner and tea provided, hours 6.00 a.m. to 6.30 p.m. Better living conditions and nature soon gave Kitty curves in all the right places, which did not escape the lustful gaze of Matt Warden when he saw her.

When she got home from work one summer's evening, Dorothy asked her to see if she could get four eggs for their supper from Matt Warden. Matt was by the door of his pigsty as she walked down the rough track at one side of the village, and his gaze sharpened as he watched her come. On reaching him, with a sweet smile, she asked, "Please, have you got four eggs to spare?"

"I haven't looked yet. I'll look for you in a minute, but come and see my new baby pigs, eleven of 'em, all beauties." And he opened the door into the sty, ushering her in. Kitty reeled nose at the odour, but was fascinated by the old sow lying grunting contentedly with eleven piglets scrambling to get a teat in their mouths.

"The old boar done a grand job with 'er, didn't 'e?" Matt boasted, then turning to her and leaning close, he

51

said, "I 'aven't noticed you courtin'. Not got a beau yet?"

"What would I want a beau for?" she said, trying to back away from the looming figure.

"Don't you know that yet? I can soon show you," and he put his two hands on her shoulders. As they stepped back outside the stye, he pressed down on her shoulders, keeping his hands there as he ushered her into the nearby fowls' cot, the pressure sending a pleasant exciting quiver through her whole body. Inside the cot, a row of hay-lined nest boxes contained five eggs. He picked them up, saying "They're for you if you give me a kiss." Kitty knew that this was very wrong, but at almost 15 years old she had more than her share of sensuality. Her half-hearted resistance was enough to fire his desire and bring Matt Warden's seduction technique into full ardour. There and then, he took her against the fowls' cot wall. Sex, without the magic satisfying ingredient of love, has an insatiable appetite. Kitty had enjoyed sex without love and, sadly for Kitty, without guilt.

Once done, Matt told Kitty to wait whilst he fetched something for her to carry the eggs in. He came back with a miniature wicker basket. "Keep the fourpence," he said, "You can bring the basket back when you come for some more," and he leerily grinned at her. Without a jot of conscience he watched her go.

She tied the four pennies tightly in her handkerchief so that they wouldn't rattle. She would keep them! She knew she must tell no-one what had happened but the secret did not disturb her. Now she knew what went on between men and women.

"You've taken your time to get those eggs," said Dorothy sharply. "And wherever have you been? There's dust and dirty cobwebs on the back of your blouse. Take it off and put a clean one on."

"I must have leaned against the cot wall while I was waiting for the eggs."

"How come you have got five when I only gave you fourpence?"

"They're a bit small, so he put an extra one in."

"Where did you get them?"

"Mr Warden's. He was just going into his fowls' cot when I was going down by there."

"I don't like that man, treats his wife like a doormat. Don't get eggs from him anymore."

Although she wouldn't mix with the other villagers, it didn't stop Dorothy from seeing what was going on and making quick judgements on what she saw. As for Kitty, now she sensed what had caused the rift between her father and cold mother, she felt no repulsion for her father. In one act, Kitty had emerged from an ignorant chrysalis with the budding wings of a nymphomaniac butterfly.

As Kitty went home Matt Warden went in for his evening meal. The cottage living room was in a muddle, clothes hung from a line strung in front of the fireplace and the fireguard was draped with clothes airing before the fire for there had been two rainy days. Two toddlers were playing under the table and a fifteen-month-old baby slept in a pram. His heavily pregnant wife was stirring a large stew pot on the hob. He had given his boots a cursory wipe on the sack by the door, but when he put his feet on the steel fender, bits of dirt stuck to it. As his wife gave him a large basin of stew, he lewdly used his hands on her. With her own hands full, she was too worn to respond in any way.

He ate with gusto, throwing the licked bones from the stew onto the fire. When he had cleared out the basin, he grunted for another helping. A mug of tea and a lump of home-made cake followed. He then stood up, broke wind and belched a couple of times before he went back out without a thank you for his wife or any attention to his offspring.

CHAPTER
EIGHT

Kitty's employers, Mr and Mrs Haines, looked an ill-matched pair. She was a thin, neat little woman with an air of anxiety about her and he was a big florid-faced man who never spoke two words if one would do. As well as the shop, he was an accountant of sorts, doing the books for many of the businesses in the town. He sometimes worked at home and would serve in the shop if they were busy. During the slack periods, Kitty was expected to do some cleaning in the house. Her mistress was very involved with church work, which took up most of her leisure time. She had lost a baby at birth in the early part of the marriage and was told she would never be able to have another child. It had devastated her and she took to religion for comfort, and by doing so much for the church, hoped God, who could work miracles, would work one for her as she was still only 37 years old.

Monday was a slack day in the shop, and Mrs Haines decided to use the time to go to Gloucester, to the wholesalers, and to do a bit of shopping at the same time. Mr Haines stayed home that day to help in the shop if needed. Trade was very slack so Kitty told Mr Haines she would go and clean the bedroom. From the broom cupboard in the kitchen she took mop, dusters, brush and dustpan and polish. Soon she was back downstairs, saying could he please come and help her move the chest of drawers so she could clean behind it. She made sure she walked up the stairs in front of him, holding her skirt tight to her as she did so, and when he had helped her to pull the chest out she smiled at him and observed what a nice bedroom it was.

"I expect that's a comfortable bed, which side do you sleep on?" and she sprawled on the bed, legs apart, with an unmistakable invitation in her hungry eyes. Mr Haines had been a faithful husband, but had also been in the army as a young man and he knew what was being offered. The surprise of her behaviour left him no time to marshal his conscience. The unexpected temptation was too much and he took the bait. Without love or any sense of propriety, he took her. He was putting on his trousers and Kitty was still lying on the bed when Mrs Haines appeared at the door.

The shock was too great for her to speak; at first she simply could not believe her eyes, then she was choking with hurt and fury. Storming forwards, her fists raised, she screamed, "Get out of this house this minute, you slut!" and Kitty went. Kitty rightly assumed Mrs Haines would be too proud for the incident ever to be mentioned except to her husband, who would be permanently unforgiven. Downstairs, a voice shouted "Shop!" and, trying to pull herself together, Nora Haines went down to the counter. But it was obvious to the customer she was upset about something.

"Be you all right, Missus? You don't look very well to me," he asked.

"No, I've just had some very distressing news," she replied, her eyes filling with tears.

"I be sorry to 'ear that, anything we can do to help?"

"No, no, thank you just the same," and she burst into tears.

The incident was soon the talk of the town but no-one could ever get Nora Haines to say what had upset her. Many made a shrewd guess.

Kitty regretted being so careless, she must not let her mother know what had happened and she must get another job. The Haines had paid her five shillings a week and given her a late breakfast and cooked lunch and most days a cup of tea and biscuits before she went home. She walked around the town shops and looked hopefully at a sign in Miss Jenkins's small shop, "Assistant Wanted, 10 shillings per week; 8.30a.m. until 6.00p.m.," but there was no mention of food. Miss Jenkins sold ribbons, tapes, braids, and all sorts of cotton and embroidery materials, knitting wools and needles and also hand-knitted baby clothes. At 12 years old, a short-sighted but serious youngster, she had gone to work for her aunt, who had owned the shop. Over the years her sight had deteriorated and although she wore thick pebble glasses she was almost blind. It was 20 years since her aunt had died and left her the shop, but because of her familiarity with everything she had somehow managed till now.

Kitty opened the door, a bell jangled loudly, but Miss Jenkins was already behind the counter. When Kitty asked about the job, as far as she could see the girl was neat and clean in her appearance.

"Have you worked before?" she asked.

"Yes but it was a newsagent's shop. I had to be there at 6 in the morning and finished at 6.30 in the evening. It was difficult in winter because I have to walk from home."

"Can you add up bills and are you good at figures?"

"Yes, I was good at arithmetic at school, you can test me if you like," Kitty said.

"Can you get me a reference?"

"Yes," said Kitty, intending to write her own as she could see Miss Jenkins was almost blind.

"Can you knit?" Miss Jenkins asked, peering at her.

"Yes. Mother taught me to knit and crochet. She hoped I would not have to go into domestic service if I had enough skill."

"You will have to knit baby clothes for the shop when you're not busy. When can you start?"

"Tomorrow if you want," and so it was settled. Kitty told her mother she had seen the notice in Miss Jenkins's shop window and that she liked the shorter hours. With no suspicions of the truth Dorothy Dowell was rather pleased with the new job and made no demur. Kitty soon settled into her new work, for there were no male customers to distract her from her duties.

CHAPTER
NINE

A couple of years later came Granny Crook's 70th birthday. Anna made a luscious fruitcake and took it in to mark the occasion, with some bedsocks that Beth had knitted and a tin of tea from herself. Granny Crook was delighted with the gesture and bustled round, putting the kettle on the fire and getting down the tea.

"Sit down, my wench, and we'll 'ave a quick cup o'tea before the others turn up. Well, the good Lord 'ave given me my three score years and ten and to tell you the truth, Anna, I don't feel I've got all that long left. I wish I could see Lenny settled down with a nice wench who would be a good wife to him, for a better man than my Lenny never breathed."

"You've got a long time to go yet, Granny, I am sure, but I do understand how you feel. I hope I can look after my Beth for a long time yet but I doubt a husband good enough would want to marry her now she's blind, although she can do almost as much as me in the house. She can cook and knit and sew and, as you know, Granny, she's just as good a girl as your Lenny is a man."

"I agree with you, my wench, and I reckon 'er 'ould make as good a wife as any other wench and a better one than some of they flibberty gibbets in the village."

"Oh Granny," and Anna gave the old lady a hug, "Wouldn't it be wonderful if Lenny took to Beth like that?"

"Trouble is, my wench, 'im do think of 'er as 'is young, after all 'e's known her since she was born, but if it could 'appen, it would be a blessing to me as well as you."

A great burden began to lift off Anna's heart; the problem of Beth's future when she had gone was a perpetual worry at the back of her mind. Now she knew that Granny Crook felt the same as she did, her hopes began to rise. Lenny was a fully grown man, healthy and a good man with a steady job down the pit. On a couple of occasions he had walked out with one or two village girls when they came home on their annual holiday but they had found him a bit shy and bashful for a two-week courtship. He and Robin were still firm friends. Robin looked up to Lenny as an icon, for Lenny was almost a match for Robin's intelligence and sensitivity, yet had a man's vigour and health. Despite her blindness, Beth was a very comely young woman, fastidious in her person with a neat well-formed figure, lovely shining brown hair, beautiful features and a gentle good-humoured personality that could be laughing and mischievous at times.

Beth loved Lenny with all her heart but never entertained the thought of romance because of her blindness. Lenny knew her so well as a playmate and a sisterly companion that he had never thought of her in a sexual way, but now he had two well-meaning would-be matchmakers scheming to influence him in that direction. The two schemers made sure the pair were left alone as much as possible. One evening, as they sat together chatting, Lenny, to his own surprise, felt an unusual sense of tenderness towards Beth. He put his arms round her and kissed her gently on the lips. Then they both sat back, she tremulous with emotion with tears in her eyes and Lenny feeling extra protective towards her, surprised at this new feeling.

It was not long before their closeness was noticed and Anna was not surprised when, a couple of months later, and obviously thrilled, Beth told her that Lenny wanted to marry her. Anna was perhaps the happier of the two, saying, "Oh darling, Granny Crook and me will both be over the moon. I couldn't be happier for you, dear," and she hugged Beth. With Lenny's approval, Beth was given Anna's engagement ring for hers. When the news of the betrothal became known, apart from a few mothers who had hoped Lenny would choose one of their daughters, there was unanimous approval.

Held that June, it was by far the best wedding in the memory of the village. Lady Benson had the wedding gown and veil made by her own dressmaker as a gift, Anna's parents paid the wedding costs, and Anna and her mother provided a wonderful spread of food, served on a lovely sunny day. Granny Crook and her daughters bought the newly weds a gramophone and some records, for Robin had influenced Beth and Lenny in a love for music.

Because Beth was so capable in her home surroundings, Anna and Granny Crook arranged that Lenny should move in with Beth and Anna would live with Granny Crook, who was now suffering the frailties of old age. Robin, who had always been welcomed by Anna and Beth, was more than ever a welcome visitor for Beth, because despite his physical handicaps he could still make himself useful in many ways and keep an eye on her when she was in the house on her own. In the evening he and Lenny would talk for hours, putting the world to rights.

Soon their talk had a background of clicking knitting needles as, to everyone's joy, Beth was pregnant. For Anna it seemed some happiness and meaning had come back into her life, it had become fulfilled with her family, her job where her kindly mistress gave her as much time off as possible, and above all the thought of a grandchild and the happiness it would bring to Beth. Anna's father had retired from the pit and he and Lenny managed Granny Crook's gardening as well as their own. Life was good!

But alas, there lived a snake in this rural idyll: Kitty Dowell. The demure-looking beautiful image she presented hid a voracious sexual appetite. Miss Jenkins was quite unaware of this, finding Kitty an obliging, capable assistant. One day she asked Kitty if she would deliver some skeins of white knitting wool to the young blind Mrs Crook; it would save someone a journey fetching it as she lived in the same village. Kitty was very willing; she would rather be in almost any one else's house than have her mother's company. When she got to the Crooks' cottage, Lenny was outside, stripped to the waist washing off the pit grime in a small zinc bath perched on a stool. Kitty licked her lips at the sight of his broad shoulders, rippling muscles and handsome face. He turned to smile at her, just as Beth appeared at his back. She thanked Kitty warmly for bringing the wool, and took her hand saying, "I am just going to make a cup of tea when I've dried Lenny's back. Would you like to step in and have one too?"

"That would be lovely. Is there anything I can do to help?"

"No, no, thank you. I can manage," and she led Kitty into the warm little room, and set her in a chair by the fire, saying she would just be a minute. Kitty sat and looked round, feeling what a contrast this was to her mother's Spartan scrubbed home. Despite Beth's blindness, there were cushioned chairs, ornaments on the mantelshelf, pictures, pots of flowers on the windowsill. She was very impressed with these, but far more impressed by the male of the house. At that moment, he came in to fetch fresh hot water from the kettle on the hob to finish his ablutions in the privacy of the scullery. Forced into this close proximity, Lenny blushed at the way she openly looked him over. He felt embarrassed and flattered at the same time. Had she been ashamed of her behaviour, Kitty would have blushed too, but it was not shame she felt, just a desire to have the man.

Kitty was amazed at Beth's dexterity. As though she could see, she had known just how much milk to put in the cup and when to stop pouring. It was obvious Lenny's home-coming meal was about to be dished up so Kitty got up to go, very happy to take the money for the wool and an order for some more to be delivered the following Thursday.

When she duly arrived with the new wool, much to her disappointment the object of her desires was on the late shift at the pit. She stayed to have a cup of tea and a piece of cake and spoke a little to Robin, who was keeping Beth company, fuelling his devotion. There was no order for more wool, but fate played into Kitty's hands. Miss Jenkins decided to sell off all the odd coloured skeins of wool at less than half price so Kitty bought several skeins and called at Beth's with them to be knitted into squares for a blanket as a gift to the baby.

This kind, unexpected gesture pleased Beth and Lenny so much that Beth suggested Kitty might like to come and spend Thursday evenings with them. Kitty said she would love to. Even if Lenny was on late shift, it would be better than being in her cold home. She wanted Lenny and she meant to have him, no matter what, and this was an open invitation to her. Anna had brought home from the big house discarded games of Ludo, playing cards and snakes and ladders, and the young people played these while chatting about everything under the sun. One night on the way home she bumped into Matt Warden shutting up his fowls for the night. At once he made a play for her, but this time she refused his advances; her lust was now centred on Lenny.

CHAPTER
TEN

For Robin, infatuated by Kitty's blue eyes and pretty manners, life was made richer by these Thursday evenings when they played games whilst Beth sat content to knit. Some weeks went by, and Robin went up to Beth's in the late morning taking some of his mother's home-made brawn sandwiches for his and Beth's lunch. Granny Crook, who had been keeping Beth company, was glad to hobble back next door to do a few little chores. Beth looked vulnerable, now very big with child, and Robin felt profound pity for her. He had overheard enough conversations on the subject of childbirth to make him marvel at what woman went through to perpetuate the species. He sensed a sadness in Beth, and asked with concern, "You feeling all right, Beth?"

She sighed, and attempted a smile, "Yes, I'm all right, Robin, but I'm worried about Lenny."

"What do you mean, worried about Lenny?"

"He's changed, Robin, he seems worried about something, and he spoke sharp to me the other day. Oh Robin, perhaps I shouldn't have let him marry me."

"Now, Beth, this is absolute nonsense. I can imagine he's worried about you and longing for the baby to come, or he might have hit a bad seam at work. You know they don't get paid anything for the stone they get out. I'm sure it's nothing to do with you though I'm surprised he spoke sharp to you." But Robin was concerned and thought he must keep an eye on the situation. He kept her company until Lenny came home from his early shift at 2.30p.m. and he couldn't help noticing Lenny didn't make his usual loving fuss of Beth. He left, feeling disturbed, and avoided going home. Instead, he hobbled down to the bottom of the village to the main road. The pub was situated there opposite a largish piece of grass. Those miners who hadn't got any pence to go to the pub and buy drink used this as an outdoor social club. They had built a rough seat from branches, and a grassy area was marked out as a quoits pitch. Men gathered round, sitting on their haunches, played quoits and engaged in men's talk — sex, politics, their jobs, their wives and the great mystery of womankind.

Now and again Robin would take his stick and hobble down to the seat for some company. The banter, the games and the impromptu wrestling and boxing matches emphasised Robin's disabilities but he was glad to find a seat by Josh Webley, an old retired miner greatly respected and liked by the whole village.

"Nice to see you, lad," observed Josh as he patted the seat next to him. "We could 'ave done with you at our place yesterday evening. That granddaughter of ours, Emily, is a right clever little wench. Twelve years old, top o' the class at school and the questions she comes out with. 'Tis young Robin you want to ask, we told 'er.

Yes, my boy, a good brain like yours is a wonderful blessing to 'ave." Robin's spirits rose. A couple of men were playing quoits and a bunch of young miners were squatting on their haunches chatting and laughing.

Partly because of his physical disability and partly due to the influence this had on his character, for a young man of 20 years Robin was quite a prude. When some lewd guffaws broke out from the young men, the others stopped to listen. One of these young men was describing in crude detail an amorous encounter he had enjoyed in the woods the previous evening. Robin paid little attention until the speaker said the enthusiastic object of his salacious attentions was Kitty Dowell. A wave of fury that the lying young braggart should say her name came over Robin. He took his walking stick and hobbled over to the grinning speaker, then with a strength he did not know he possessed, he hit him on the jaw with his fist, sending the fellow sprawling on his back in a state of utter surprise.

"What the 'ell, what's up with you anyway! You're lucky I don't give you a fistful back for that."

"You're a foul mouthed liar and ought to be castrated. You're not fit to utter that girl's name."

At this remark there was some ribald laughter and comment, and this response made Robin feel almost too weak to get back to sit by Josh on the seat.

"I know you meant well, my boy, but I'm afeared you be in the wrong here. 'Tis common knowledge that the wench 'ave gone to the bad. A lot of the children 'ave reckoned they've seen her layin' in the ferns wi' different men, Matt Warden among 'em and our son

Jock reckons 'er's bin pesterin' 'im and 'im a married man wi' three young 'uns. 'Tis a sort of illness some wenches get when they can't leave men alone. 'Er mother would kill 'er if she knowed, but it's allus the nearest as is the last to know. Such wenches be a nuisance, they spread a lot o' trouble and disease and causes poor diseased children to be born. It's a dirty trick nature plays on women sometimes."

The old man's words seared Robin's spirits, taking the strength out of him. Human beings, from the highly cultured to the primitive in the jungle, need their gods to look up to. The human spirit in all of us needs someone to respect and love, and give love and respect back. It helps to balance the "slings and arrows of outrageous fortune". But Robin's emotional world was crumbling with the knowledge he had just acquired. He could not bear the thoughts that were torturing his mind.

He remembered how Kitty always sat next to Lenny when they played games on Thursday evenings, how she would playfully tap his hand and how Lenny would seem flushed and even excited and nowadays seemed to be more groomed on these evenings, his hair well brushed and a fresh clean shirt on. Was Lenny falling victim to this rose with the maggoty centre? Oh it must not be, but things were adding up in his mind. Recently when Anna had been given the evening off, Lenny had said he was going to see a pit mate and went out for the evening, a thing he never did as a rule. Oh no, no, no, Robin's mind begged but his suspicions would not go away. Beth must never know. On Thursday he would watch for any signs of over-familiarity. If there was any truth in this awful scenario, somehow he would put a stop to it.

Lenny had sown no wild oats in his youth, and subtle encouragement had led him into marrying Beth, whom he loved dearly. Of late, because of the coming baby and out of concern for Beth, he had put his desires on hold. But he had become bewildered by the effect of the wanton beauty who had somehow insinuated herself into his household, creating longing that overcame his scruples. She had made it plain that she wanted him, and to his disgust his body responded, giving him no peace. How could he be like this when he loved Beth with all his heart and mind? Kitty was only interested in his good looks and manly virility, her blatant sexuality had hypnotized him, and when she tapped his hand in playful scolding over the board games, he felt a charge of desire that shook his very being. She was an enslaver by nature, and he had become enslaved.

On the next Thursday evening it was difficult for Robin to show his ordinary demeanour. He noticed how enticingly Kitty was dressed, with her hair curled, and he could smell her perfume. He watched her eyes as she spoke to Lenny and the truth began to weigh like lead in his heart. He often felt the problem of carnality in his own loins but Lenny was married to someone special and with forthcoming fatherhood, how could Lenny, his icon of manliness and decency, fall so low? His own attraction to the bewitcher had changed into dislike and even hate, which made it difficult for Robin to speak to her. Pity for Beth, sitting as usual with her knitting, swollen and awkward in the last stages of pregnancy, welled up in him. For Beth's sake he must act normally.

It was usual for some potatoes to be put in the side of the oven to bake for refreshment. When they were cooked, Lenny would cut them open and put some cheese and salt and pepper on them. This evening Robin felt too choked to eat anything and he said he wasn't hungry. Whilst Lenny made a pot of tea and Kitty set the cups out, Robin noticed that she touched him at every opportunity, but that Lenny flinched as she did so. When they had finished their tea, they resumed their game of snakes and ladders. Kitty kept the scores in a small notebook she brought with her. When Robin shook the dice it rolled off the table beside him, and bending down to pick it up he was in time to see Kitty remove her hand from the top of Lenny's thigh. The deep flush on Robin's cheeks when he sat up again was due more to the treachery than the effort. He felt like shaking Lenny to his senses and edged his chair away from Kitty, feeling an indescribable rage for her. His mind went back to the beautiful waiflike girl he had first seen in Chapel. How could she have descended into a wanton slut?

He was glad when it was time to go home, deciding he would confront Kitty Dowell and somehow shame her out of this impasse. As he turned to pat Beth's head and say goodnight, he saw Kitty put a piece of her notepad under the lamp. Staying behind the others, he picked it up and put it in his pocket. He would delay

71

confronting her until he could read it. Forced by politeness to see Kitty home, by the time they walked to her cottage door Robin had not spoken a word.

"What's the matter, the cat got your tongue?" she said.

He didn't answer, leaving her standing at her door, and went on to his own home. He turned up the wick of the paraffin lamp in the middle of the table and read the piece of paper. It said, "Quarry Dell, eight o'clock tomorrow." Robin remembered Beth saying that Anna was going round to sit with her the next evening. That bitch Kitty! She knew Lenny would get away and see her. Well, he thought, Kitty Dowell was in for a big surprise for it was he who would be at Quarry Dell. Quarry Dell was rarely frequented. The top of the quarry was a few feet from the main road, about half a mile from the village. Its jagged sides dropped steeply down to the valley road which branched out from the bottom of the village. At the bottom of the quarry lay a deep, black, stagnant pool where the occasional sheep drowned after losing its footing. Parents warned their children to keep away from the area. It had a lonely morbid air and was a melancholy spot, despite the little wooded dell at its summit. Robin made up his mind to make a superhuman effort to be there at eight o'clock.

Fate played into his hands when his mother observed that she would let the village butcher know that she wanted to order a joint of beef for Sunday dinner as her eldest son and his wife were coming. The butcher's house was the last one on the row straggling up the main road on the way to the quarry. "I'll take the order tomorrow evening," Robin offered. His mother thought it was too far for him to struggle to, but he persisted, remonstrating that he was not that handicapped. Eventually she demurred so as not to hurt his feelings.

The next evening, he started out after his tea and was indeed exhausted by the time he reached the butcher's house. They were surprised to see him, but welcomed him in and gave him a cup of tea, talking to him as they finished their meal. Had they seen Robin continue down the main road, they would have been astonished. Robin had an iron will in his frail body and somehow, with many rests along the way, he made it to the quarry top. He leant his exhausted frame against a tree a few feet from the edge, where the idea occurred to him to throw himself over the edge to end his emotional and physical misery. But an opposing thought about how it would cause pain to his mother and would not help Lenny stopped him from acting on his thoughts.

It was just getting dusk when Kitty appeared. "What on earth are you doing here? Did Lenny send you?" she demanded on seeing the crooked figure rather than the tall man she expected.

"No, Lenny didn't send me, I took your note before he could see it."

"You took my note! You sly little rat! Well, you can mind you own business! Don't come the goody goody with me, you men are all the same, you as well if you could be. You are all only interested in one thing. I'll bet you wouldn't say no to lying down in the dell with me for a bit. I could give you a good time, then you could keep you mouth shut about Lenny and me!"

Robin could not believe his ears. Fury, disillusionment and hate welled up to choke him with tears. He shouted, "You slut, it *is* my business. Beth and Lenny are my friends, you keep away from them. What kind of woman are you to betray a woman like Beth? You are a fiend and a hypocrite and you aren't fit to clean her shoes."

"You try and stop me! If she can't, you certainly won't!" she screamed back.

At that his temper broke and he strode towards her with his eyes blazing with fury and his stick upraised to hit her. She stepped back, suddenly scared of him. Her foot caught in some undergrowth, and she grabbed at a lower branch of the tree to save herself. It snapped off in her hand and she lost her footing again and fell backwards into the quarry. Her scream of horror as she fell was only answered by the hooting of an owl in the dark and lonely forest.

Robin stood in horror, thinking Oh God, what had he done. He had felt murderous hate and rage, but had not intended to send her to her death. Perhaps she wasn't dead. Perhaps she had survived the fall and would manage to climb out of the deep murky water. He knew she couldn't swim, only a few daredevil lads taught themselves in the pool by the brickworks. The girls never went near them for fears of reprisal as the lads often stripped off for their water antics. A feeling of isolation was not unusual for Robin but now, with only his conscience for company, he was utterly bereft. His mind was in such turmoil it almost blotted out the painfulness of his progress. Was it him or the hand of God that had sent Kitty to her death? Logic told him that was nonsense; what sort of god would make such flawed creatures only to find ways of killing them? Somehow he had to find the strength to retrace his steps on the main road, then go down the valley to the quarry pool. Sobbing with the pain in mind and body, he made his way slowly down to the pool.

Was Kitty Dowell still alive? She was young — perhaps she had scrabbled out of the pool. Maybe he would meet her on the way down the valley, but all was silent except for the sound of his own laboured breathing and the occasional hoot of an owl. His eyes grew accustomed to the darkness and he peered into the gloom, though he could not escape the morbid thought that he had killed her and that Lenny and Beth would escape her evil intentions. At last he arrived but the pool was eerily smooth, black and sinister. He called Kitty's name over and over again, his voice echoing in the dark. No answer came.

CHAPTER
ELEVEN

When he arrived home, his mother was waiting by the gate with a coat over her nightdress. She caught hold of him, saying "Wherever have you been? I've been worried sick about you."

"Sorry, Mother," he replied, leaning heavily on his stick with weariness. "I walked a bit too far and got so tired I had to find somewhere to lie down and went to sleep. It was dark when I woke."

"I told you it was too far to the butcher's, let alone going into the woods as well. It's done you no good. Anyway, you look worn out and as if you've seen a ghost. Have your supper, though it's got dry in the oven. I'll put the kettle over what's left of the fire and make you a cup of cocoa. It will help you to sleep. Get up to bed as soon as you've finished."

It was a long time before he could face his bed and sleep would not come. He lay staring up into the dark, his mind running in circles. Was Kitty at home trying to explain herself to her mother? Or was she lying dead at the bottom of the quarry pool? It was dawn before exhaustion closed his eyes.

★   ★   ★

Dorothy Dowell knew that she did not enjoy a normal motherly relationship with Kitty; she did not like her daughter who was too much like her father. She had noticed the same expression in Kitty's eyes when a man was about as her husband had for another woman but she had no inkling of Kitty's promiscuity, believing that her careful training of her child had been effective. Kitty never stayed in with her mother if she could help it. In the summer she made the excuse she loved to be out in the forest and would bring bundles of kindling wood in with her. In the winter she said she was in different neighbours' cottages but the rule was that Kitty must be indoors by nine in the evening at the very latest. The clock was almost on 9 o'clock and Dorothy Dowell began to get irritable; she was tired and wanted her bed, for she had to be up early to go to her job as a cleaner in the town. At 10.15 she was very angry.

She sat on the wooden chair and put up another to put her legs on. Lots of villagers never locked their doors but she did and would have locked Kitty out, only the neighbours might hear Kitty knocking and start talking. She dozed off and the clock said nearly midnight when she woke up. There was still no sign of Kitty. Dorothy Dowell thought the sly hussy had come home and sneaked up to bed without wakening her mother, but she would now get her punishment for this behaviour. With her right hand tingling to chastise the miscreant, she went up to Kitty's bedroom. It was empty and fear overtook the anger. There was nothing taken from her bedroom, her clean blouse for the next day was folded neatly on the back of a chair. There had been no hint of her running away in her behaviour, so had she been seeing a man? The idea now grew more likely. Dorothy Dowell thought, My God, had she been abducted or even worse? Perhaps she would still turn up, all the worse for some unforeseen experience. Or maybe — Dorothy's blood ran cold at the sudden thought — maybe she had been murdered.

Pride kept her from knocking at any village doors at such an hour, but if in the morning Kitty hadn't returned, she would call on young blind Mrs Crook as she knew Kitty was very friendly with her. Maybe she had stayed overnight with her. The morning came but no Kitty. Beth was very surprised to have a visit from Mrs Dowell but told her she had not seen Kitty since Thursday evening when she seemed perfectly all right. There was no alternative; Dorothy Dowell had to report her missing daughter to the police. When a policeman was seen calling at her house, village curiosity became boundless and the truth had to come out, Kitty Dowell had gone missing!

Some men in the village grew uncomfortable. They were not guilty of anything criminal but the police were nosey buggers, they could find out who had been with Kitty Dowell and it would cause ructions with wives and mothers. Lenny was very perturbed. The evening she had gone missing, he had found an excuse to go out, saying he was wondering why Robin hadn't called in. In truth, in the dark he had hung around like a tomcat, hoping to see Kitty. Shame for himself and concern for her made it hard for him to conceal his moodiness. Kitty had groomed him, ripe for the picking with her bold underhand coquetry. Could he be blamed somehow for her disappearance? He would look at Beth and be filled with self-loathing and remorseful thoughts.

The police scoured every inch of terrain round the village, investigated the disused mines and dragged the streams and pools. They questioned every male in the village, resulting in a few furious rows between some husbands and wives, but no evidence came to light to charge anyone with her disappearance. Suspicion attacked the village like a virus. Matt Warden was high on the list of suspects, but no man escaped. The village women seethed with angry gossip at what had been going on under their noses. Robin's mind was in torture, he was ready to accept the blame for what had happened but feared somehow Lenny would become implicated. Also, he knew the scandal would break his poor mother's heart. He still felt it was a blessing that he had seen Kitty's note and prevented Lenny from a foolish action.

Two weeks later, after a long and painful labour, Beth gave birth to a beautiful seven-pound baby son. Lenny was home from work during the last hours of Beth's labour. Her moans, as he paced the floor downstairs, made him groan with his own helplessness and remorse. He could hear Anna and the midwife coaxing her to be brave. Oh how unworthy he was of Beth. There was no one he could share the burden with, not even Robin, for Robin would never understand. "Oh God, please help me!" he heard Beth cry, and "God help me!" Lenny's agony echoed. At last he heard a baby cry and the joyous sounds of Anna and the midwife bustling about to make Beth and the baby comfortable. Anna placed the bathed and night-gowned baby in Beth's arms, then ran downstairs to make tea and tell Lenny to go up to meet his new son.

The excitement of expecting a baby is one thing; to actually see the flesh and blood itself is far beyond imagining, and feelings of gratitude, love and pride were all too much for Lenny. When the women came back upstairs with tea and food they pretended not to notice that Lenny was crying.

There was joy all over the village at this birth. Between Anna's parents, Granny Crook, Anna, Lenny and Robin, Beth always had someone with her. The aura of love that surrounded the baby made him thrive and coo with contentment. The coming of the child brought a new dimension to their marriage. Grateful for their precious co-achievement came the desire to make each other happy and although they had never heard of the Karma Sutra, Cupid taught them his wiles.

It was a wonderful marriage, marred for Lenny only by his remembrance of Kitty Dowell. Two years on and a baby girl was welcomed with equal joy. As a gift to Beth's beloved Dad, Anna suggested they call her Eirwhin, and Beth and Lenny readily agreed. By this time Granny Crook had become very frail. Climbing the stairs to her bed exhausted her so Lenny carried her bed downstairs and Anna made the little parlour into a bed-sitting room for her. Granny was, with the approval of her two daughters, leaving the cottage to Lenny, so it was decided to make the two cottages into one dwelling by knocking the wall down between the two back sculleries. This left a room upstairs for her great-grandson, two-year-old Robin. They had named him Robin James and the proudest person at the christening had been Robin. Later on a baby girl, Mary, shared Anna's room, for the smaller cottage only had one bedroom and a small landing area.

Autumn came and with it the all too often hungry scoured the ground for nuts from the rare sweet chestnut trees and the hazels among the oaks. They carried jam jars and basins to gather the blackberries that grew in nearby clumps. Despite being told by their parents to keep away from the quarry, a couple of the older lads had gone there to gather luscious berries from the fine bushes that grew near the pool, now very deep from a wet summer and autumn. Being boys they had to try and skim stones across the surface of the pool. One of them noticed a boulder perched precariously on a jagged protuberance nearly halfway up the quarry side.

"Let's go and push that bugger into the pool!"

"No fear. You might lose your hold and fall in."

"Well, I can swim so I will be all right!"

"You wouldn't be all right if you went 'ome soaked to the skin. You'd get a good hiding for just being here."

"You be a coward. I'm gonna push that thing into the water. You just watch."

As agile as a goat, but with care and a boy's natural ability, he reached the boulder. It was huge, but so finely balanced that a couple of good shoves sent it hurtling down with a rattle of stones to land with a huge splash in the pool. As it sank, something came up out of the water and caught on a dead branch sticking out from the bank. It looked like an item of clothing. Curious as to what it was they had found, three long sticks were found, tied together with their socks, and used to tease the garment off the branch. When recovered, it provoked sniggering laughter.

"It's a pair of drawers!"

"Chuck 'em back in!"

"No fear. Let's take them back to show the others. We can tease the girls. Look they've got lace round the bottom."

With a pail full of blackberries in one hand and a stick draped with the sodden remains of the drawers in the other, they sniggered and laughed their way home. They were just nearing the village when they met Ernie Madson coming into the woods to answer a call of nature. Seeing the little procession, he called out, "What've you got there, boys?"

They could hardly speak for laughing. Waving their find like a flag, they finally got out, "We found these in the quarry pool. We're going to tease the girls with them."

Despite the poor state of the garment, Ernie recognised it, and he returned home a very thoughtful man. Villages are the worst places in which to keep secrets, and the boys had been very blatant in their use of the garment to tease their female enemies. Rumours of their find eventually reached the police, and they returned to investigate the quarry pool more carefully. This time they found Kitty Dowell.

When the police arrived back in the village, speculation abounded. The women concluded Kitty must have got herself pregnant and drowned herself out of fear of her mother. To be driven to such despair so young made the most hard-hearted and moral feel pity for her. For a while the village had a small share of morbid fame, for the case even made it into the national newspapers. In the pit breaks men talked of little else; housewives gathered in little groups, chewing over this tragic mystery, and neglecting their housework. Some of the villagers were puzzled. The police were supposed to have dragged all the ponds around the village. There was the suggestion that she had been murdered and her body dumped in the pond after the police had dragged it, but this theory was dismissed as very unlikely. It was concluded that the police must either have missed the pool, or made a poor effort at the job.

All the men were questioned again by the police, including Robin, although his physical frailty and good character excluded him from being a possible suspect in their minds. There was shock again when Mr Dowell came home for the funeral. He did not stay and Kitty's mother, more grim faced and eccentrically lonely than ever, moved away to Kent where her sister and brother-in-law lived. The saga of the Dowells stayed in the village history, especially in the tortured heart and mind of Robin.

Although chapel people, the funeral was held in the church as it could hold more. There were not many tears of pity, but much discussion about the mysterious drowning. Now, as well as the burden of his twisted spine, Robin carried the burden of his conscience. There was no-one with whom he could share this burden. It would be cruel to add to his mother's worries on his behalf and telling Lenny was out of the question. He sought for an answer in the logic of his thoughts, but no answer came to his questions. Why had Kitty Dowell, that exquisite, virginal girl, grown into a wanton, evil creature? Why had Lenny, who had so many blessings, yielded to her temptations? Why was there a blight for every growing plant? Why was nature so cruel? Because there was so much beauty in life, must we have ugliness to be able to appreciate the beauty? He could find no answers and despite all his efforts to hide his distress, Robin grew quiet and withdrawn. Lenny had rightly guessed some time ago that Robin had been hopelessly bewitched by Kitty Dowell and so was the more upset when her real character was revealed. He had created out of Kitty Dowell an icon for his own emotional needs, but worshipped at the heart of a scented flower only to discover it had maggots of self-destruction in its petals. Yet Lenny felt he could not reveal these thoughts to Robin without pouring salt on the raw wound in his heart. They were both victims of a calculating woman, though Lenny realised that he was a guilty one.

Life in the village went on, with its usual share of mishaps, heads became greyer, limbs grew stiff with rheumatism but as the old ones faded, new babies came along, bringing energy and fresh sap to the human season. Then misery hit the village with a virulent sort of flu that turned into pneumonia. It killed 12-year-old Edith Newall who had been chesty and weak from birth. It also stuck down Bill Moore, an 83-year-old bachelor. As well as working in the mines he had always run a large flock of sheep on the free grazing areas in the forest. He had been a parsimonious spender, and it was reckoned he had a hoard of gold sovereigns hidden somewhere. There was great speculation about who would get their hands on them. Mrs Howe lost her new baby, but as it was her twelfth some thought it was a blessing in disguise.

Anna was grateful each day that her family escaped but despite the fact Robin's mother dosed him with her herbal brews, rubbed his twisted chest with goose grease and made him special nourishing gruels, Robin caught it. His already frail body and tortured mind lowered his resistance. His mother went to tell Beth and Lenny but asked Lenny to keep away in case he brought the virus home and gave it to the children. Reluctantly Lenny agreed. A few days later, in a very distressed state, she knocked on Lenny's door.

"Oh my boy, I don't like to ask you but Robin's very ill. I think my boy's dying and he keeps asking for you. Can you come?"

"Of course I'll come," said Lenny.

He was not prepared for the sight of Robin lying still in his bed; a lump came into his throat. Robin's hands lay on the white counterpane as thin as a chicken's claws, and his dark sunken eyes, already marked with death, looked too big for his emaciated face. Lenny sat on a chair by the bedside in the spotlessly clean little bedroom and took Robin's hands between his own large strong pit-scarred ones. Out of his own eyes shone a deep brotherly love for this life-long friend struggling to breathe.

Robin whispered, "I have something to tell you, Lenny," then with a struggle, gasping and resting for breath, his hands encased by Lenny's, Robin told him of the events that evening long before at Quarry Dell. At first Lenny thought he was delirious. How could he have found the strength to walk all the way to Quarry Dell and been moved enough to scare someone like Kitty Dowell, causing her to plunge to her death. Yet he knew how strong Robin's character and will were.

"I wanted to own up to what I did, Lenny, but I was afraid you would be involved and it would break Beth's heart if she had known. If you want to hand me in, please wait till Mother's gone before you tell the police, or let it bide if you'd rather."

Lenny had been well aware of Robin's adulation of Kitty although the subject had never been spoken between them. Gratitude, horror, sadness and admiration for his friend, this crippled friend who was so far superior to him, overcame Lenny.

"Oh Rob, forgive me," he sighed. As he did so Robin look at him, with love in his eyes, then his head fell back, his eyes rolled to show only the whites, and Robin was dead. Gripped by emotions almost too difficult to bear, Lenny sat motionless in shock as Robin's mother came in the room. He looked at her with haggard eyes.

"I be afeared him's gone, went like a lamb. I hope I shall do the same, but him 'ave took a bit of me with him, you had a wonderful son there. I wish I was half the man that he was."

"Oh Lenny, it was my wish that he would die first for who would look after him when I be gone, but I shall miss him so, 'twas him that kept me going. Now if you go downstairs, when I've seen to my precious boy, I'll make you a cup of tea."

In common grief they drank their tea and wept and talked about Robin. Very slowly, with leaden legs, Lenny walked up the steep path to his home. By the time he reached it he had decided that he would not tell the police — he would let the matter bide. It would be best that Robin's memory was not associated with such as Kitty Dowell. He himself must bear his guilt to the end of his days. He didn't deserve Beth and his children but he vowed to himself he would never let them down again.

The death of Robin brought a sad vacuum into their lives. He had shared their hearth and their hearts over so many years. Without him Robin's mother was bereft so Beth and Lenny would encourage her to come up to them for company. There is nothing that eases a bereaved heart so much as being able to share memories of the lost one, to weep together and to laugh together, to lessen the burden with the sharing. Anna and Granny Cook joined in, and Granny Cook grew very close to Robin's mother, many evenings sitting with her talking about the old days, the lost ones, and finding delight in the company of the two grandchildren. With Anna as head of the family, they all fitted in as comfortably as peas in a pod, making the most of what life had to offer, but as time passed, increasingly Lenny realized what a superhuman effort Robin had made on his behalf, both physically and emotionally. It was a shadow for the rest of what was a very fulfilled and contented life.

Also available in ISIS Large Print:

Charlotte Fairlie

D. E. Stevenson

Charlotte Fairlie is a successful, elegant career woman. Still in her 20s, she has landed a job as headmistress of her old school. She is admired and liked by both staff and pupils — but she begins to feel there is something missing in her well-organised life.

Then one summer she goes to stay with a young pupil on the remote Scottish Isle of Targ. In the romantic atmosphere of the Highlands, anything can happen — and even the cool, efficient Charlotte surprises herself . . .

ISBN 0-7531-7614-9 **(hb)**
ISBN 0-7531-7615-7 **(pb)**

The Frozen Lake

Elizabeth Edmondson

The year of 1936 is drawing to a close. Winter grips
Westmoreland and causes a rare phenomenon: the lakes
freeze. For two local families, the Richardsons and the
Grindleys, this will bring unexpected upheaval as the
frozen lake entices long-estranged siblings and children
to return home for the holiday season.

Childhood friendships are rekindled, old rivalries
resurface and new relationships sparkle with possibili-
ties. Everyone's keen to put aside their troubles —
money worries, love tangles, career problems, domestic
rifts — and enjoy themselves skating while they can.
But one visitor carries the seed of violence and not even
the redoubtable matriarch of the Richardson clan can
prevent the carefully buried secrets of the past from
reappearing and transforming everything.

ISBN 0-7531-7429-4 **(hb)**
ISBN 0-7531-7430-8 **(pb)**

Prejudice and Pride

Winifred Foley

The Forest of Dean in the early 20th century is a place of great beauty, but also of great harshness and poverty. Kezzie and Tess know both aspects, particularly Kezzie whose father is arrested for sheep-stealing, her family being thrown out to face a hostile world. Tess in the meantime follows the tradition of the Forest girls and goes into service in Bristol.

Kezzie is "discovered" by a theatrical impresario and goes on to become a world-famous singer; Tess meets and marries the man of her dreams, raises a family and endures long years of hard work lightened by happy family life. Kezzie is successful, but love has always turned to ashes and she has no-one to love and be loved in return. Tess, despite the death of her husband, has a supportive and loving family.

But all through their lives, each looks back with longing to their early friendship and the happy days as children in the Forest. It is only pride, and the prejudice of pride, that stops them from seeking one another — until the longing for their childhood home leads each to buy a house in the Forest.

ISBN 0-7531-7223-2 (hb)
ISBN 0-7531-7224-0 (pb)

The Marigold Field

Diane Pearson

Through the vibrant years of the early part of the century — from 1896 to 1919 — lived the Whitmans, the Pritchards and the Dances, whose lives were destined to be intertwined . . .

Jonathan Whitman, his cousin Myra, Anne Louise Pritchard and the enormous Pritchard clan to which she belonged, saw the changing era and the incredible events of a passing age — an age of great poverty and great wealth, of the Boer War and social reform, of straw boaters, feather boas and the music hall.

Throughout all of this is the story of one woman's consuming love and of a jealous obsession that threatened to destroy the very man she adored . . .

ISBN 0-7531-7331-X (hb)
ISBN 0-7531-7332-8 (pb)